Parents and Caregivers,

Stone Arch Readers are designed to provide enjoyable reading experiences, as well as opportunities to develop vocabulary, literacy skills, and comprehension. Here are a few ways to support your beginning reader:

• Talk with your child about the ideas addressed in the story.

• Discuss each illustration, mentioning the characters, where they are, and what they are doing.

• Read with expression, pointing to each word. You may want to read the whole story through and then revisit parts of the story to ensure that the meanings of words or phrases are understood.

• Talk about why the character did what he or she did and what your child would do in that situation.

• Help your child connect with characters and events in the story.

Remember, reading with your child should be fun, not forced. Each moment spent reading with your child is a priceless investment in his or her literacy life.

Gail Saunders-Smith, Ph.D.

Stone Arch Readers

are published by Stone Arch Books
a Capstone Imprint
1710 Roe Crest Drive
North Mankato, Minnesota 56003
www.capstonepub.com

Library of Congress Cataloging-in-Publication Data
Crow, Melinda Melton.
Rocky and Daisy go to the vet / by Melinda Melton Crow; illustrated by Eva Sassin.
p. cm. -- (Stone Arch readers: My two dogs)
Summary: Rocky and Daisy reluctantly visit the veterinarian.
ISBN 978-1-4342-6009-3 (library binding) -- ISBN 978-1-4342-6203-5 (pbk.)
1. Dogs--Juvenile fiction. 2. Veterinarians--Juvenile fiction. [1. Dogs--Fiction.
2. Veterinarians--Fiction.] I. Sassin, Eva, ill. II. Title.
PZ7.C88536Rpn 2013
813.6--dc23   2012047364

Reading Consultants:
Gail Saunders-Smith, Ph.D.
Melinda Melton Crow, M.Ed.
Laurie K. Holland, Media Specialist

Designer: Kristi Carlson

Printed in China by Nordica.
0413/CA21300452
032013
007226NORDF13

Rocky and Daisy
Go to the Vet

by **Melinda Melton Crow**

illustrated by **Eva Sassin**

STONE ARCH BOOKS

a capstone imprint

MY TWO DOGS

I'm Owen, and these are Rocky and Daisy, my two dogs.

ROCKY LIKES:

- Chasing squirrels

- Playing with other dogs

- Chewing things

- Running with me when I ride my bike

DAISY LIKES:

- Playing ball

- Listening to stories

- Resting on the furniture

- Eating yummy treats

Rocky and Daisy lived with
Owen and his family. They
liked to play in the backyard.

They liked to swim in the pool.

And they liked their comfy beds.

Most of all, they liked to go for rides in the van. Sometimes they went to the dog park.

Sometimes they went to the beach.

Sometimes they went to the
pet store.

One morning, Dad said,
"Let's go for a ride."

"Hooray!" shouted Rocky.

"I wonder where we are
going," said Daisy.

"I hope we are going to the beach," whispered Rocky.

"I want to go to the dog park," whispered Daisy.

They stuck their heads out
of the van windows and sniffed
the air. "I don't smell the
beach," said Rocky.

Then they drove past the dog park. Daisy sighed.

The van stopped. Daisy sniffed. "Oh, no," she said. "We are at the vet!"

Daisy and Rocky began to tremble.

"I'm not getting out of the van," said Daisy.

"I'm not either!" shouted Rocky.

It was hard to get the dogs
out of the van. Dad pulled on
Rocky's collar. Owen pulled
Daisy from behind.

"It's okay," said Owen. "It won't be that bad."

Rocky and Daisy waited for
their turn with the vet.

"You are going to like Dr. Jay,"
said Owen. "She is very nice."

But Rocky and Daisy did not believe him. They had to get away.

"Let's make a run for it,"
shouted Rocky. "Follow me,
Daisy."

Rocky ran toward the open
door. Daisy was close behind.

"Not so fast," said Dad. He quickly closed the door.

Rocky crashed into the door. Daisy piled on top of him.

"Ah, man," said Rocky.

Soon, Dr. Jay came into the room. She petted Rocky and Daisy. They slowly wagged their tails.

"Maybe this really won't be so bad," said Daisy.

Rocky and Daisy smiled a little. Dr. Jay peeked at their teeth as they smiled.

"Please put them on the table," said Dr. Jay.

Dr. Jay began to scratch their ears. "Ah, man," said Rocky. "I love having my ears scratched."

Dr. Jay checked their ears as
she scratched them.

"Who wants a treat?" asked
Dr. Jay. Both Rocky and Daisy
wanted a treat.

As they chewed their treats,
Dr. Jay gave them each a shot.
But they didn't even notice.

"Time to go home," said Dad.

Owen walked the dogs to the van. "That wasn't so bad, huh?" said Owen.

"I like Dr. Jay," said Daisy.

"Me too," said Rocky.

"She petted us and scratched our ears," said Rocky.

"She gave us treats," added Daisy.

"When can we go back to the vet?" they asked.

Dad and Owen just smiled.

THE END

STORY WORDS

comfy	sighed	scratch
sniffed	tremble	treat

Total Word Count: 443

READ MORE

ROCKY AND DAISY ADVENTURES!